To: Will

From: God

the Gift

Then the King said:
"A beautiful face is of litt[le]
[worth unle]ss there is beauty of character
[...] we shall not decide this impor[tant]
[...]on for three days."

slipper will dance

THE
GIFT

For every small
heart that needs
to know...
there's a love
deep inside you
waiting to
grow.

this heart
belongs
to

_____

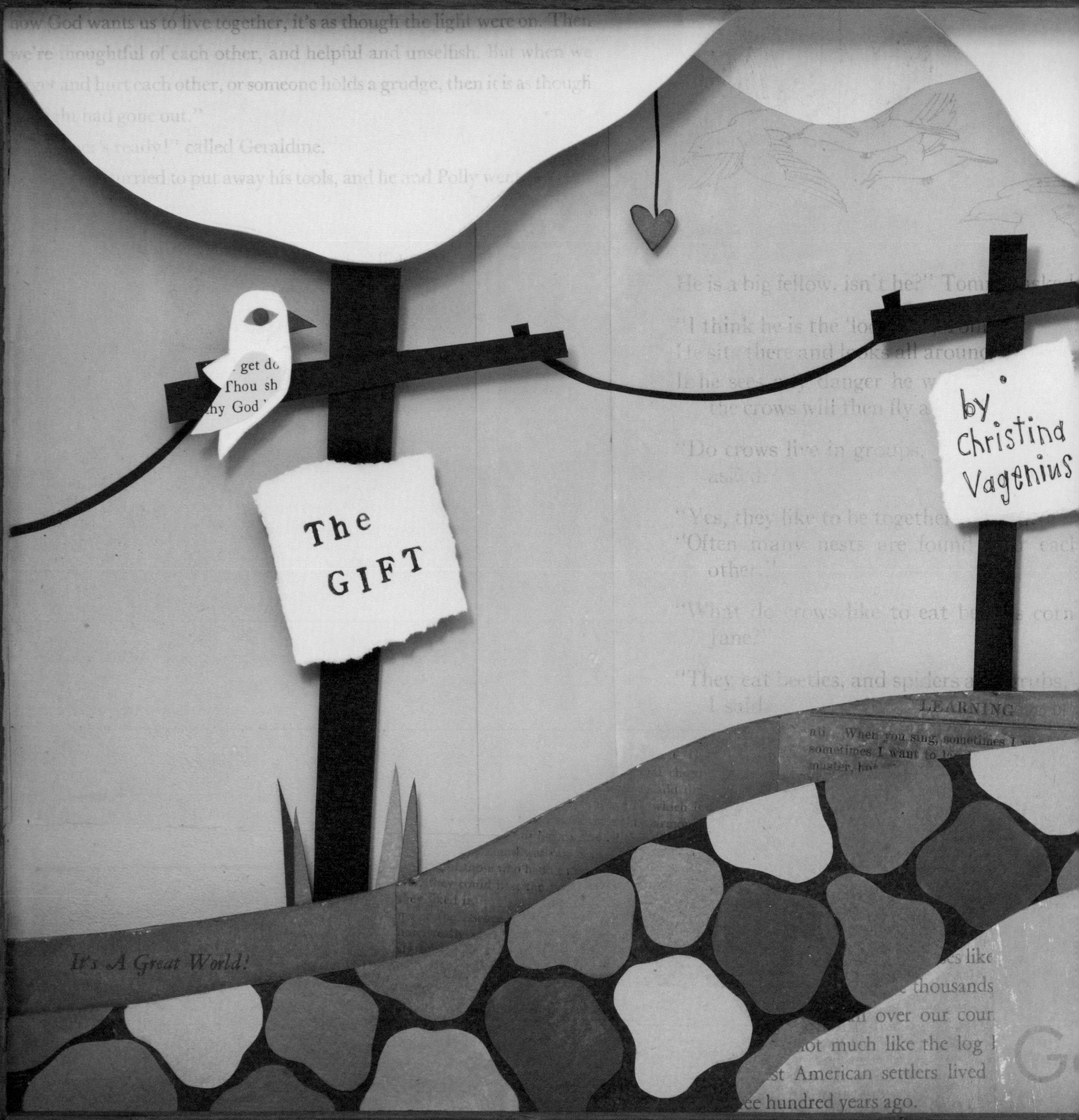
The GIFT
by Christina Vagenius
It's A Great World!

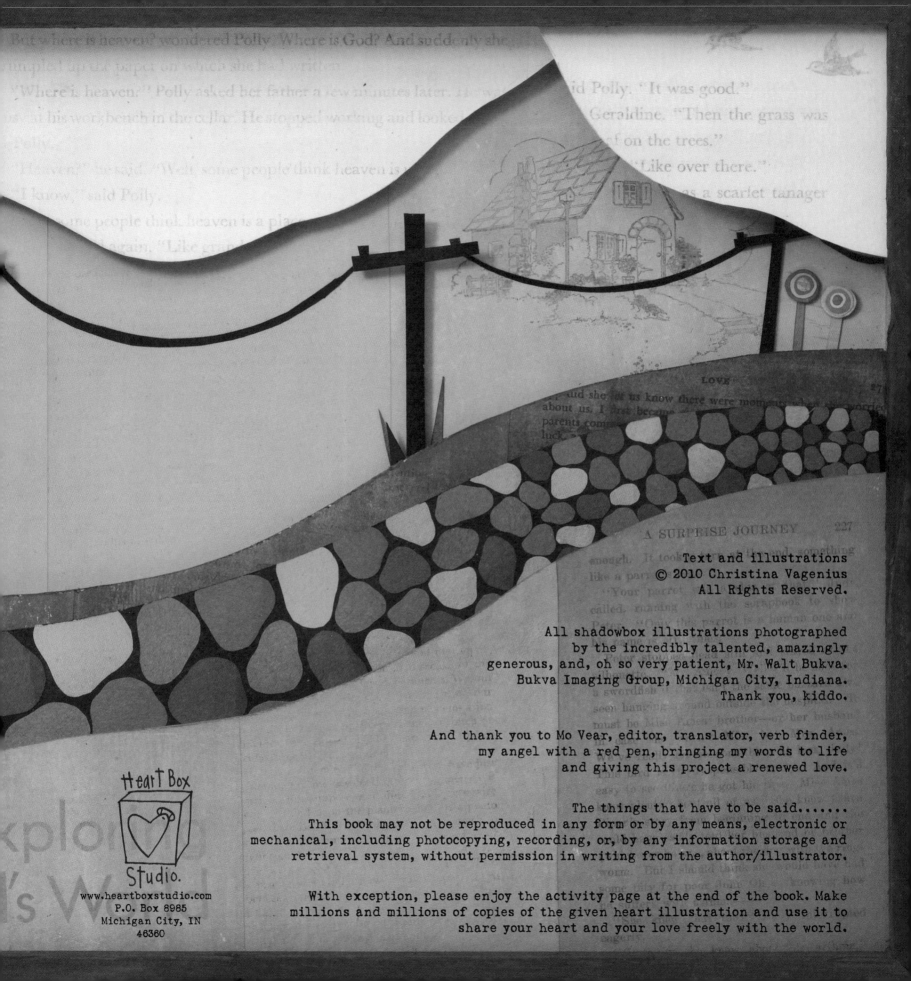

All shadowbox illustrations photographed
by the incredibly talented, amazingly
generous, and, oh so very patient, Mr. Walt Bukva.
Bukva Imaging Group, Michigan City, Indiana.
Thank you, kiddo.

And thank you to Mo Vear, editor, translator, verb finder,
my angel with a red pen, bringing my words to life
and giving this project a renewed love.

Heart Box
Studio.

www.heartboxstudio.com
P.O. Box 8985
Michigan City, IN
46360

There once was
a boy, a small
boy named Will,
who watched
from above
quiet and
still.

And so it
was, on the
day he was
born, he was
given a box,
weathered and
worn.

And there on the
box in a ribbon
of red, "The Gift,"
in black letters
was all that it said.

Will + God ♡

And there in the box, one heart made of love, one path, one home, one faithful white dove.

The boy heard a whisper,

"This is my heart, pinned to you before you depart. Given to you, so you'll always know, my love is with you wherever you go."

And the
small boy grew.
His ears opened wide
to a voice that was true.

And this small voice whispered,

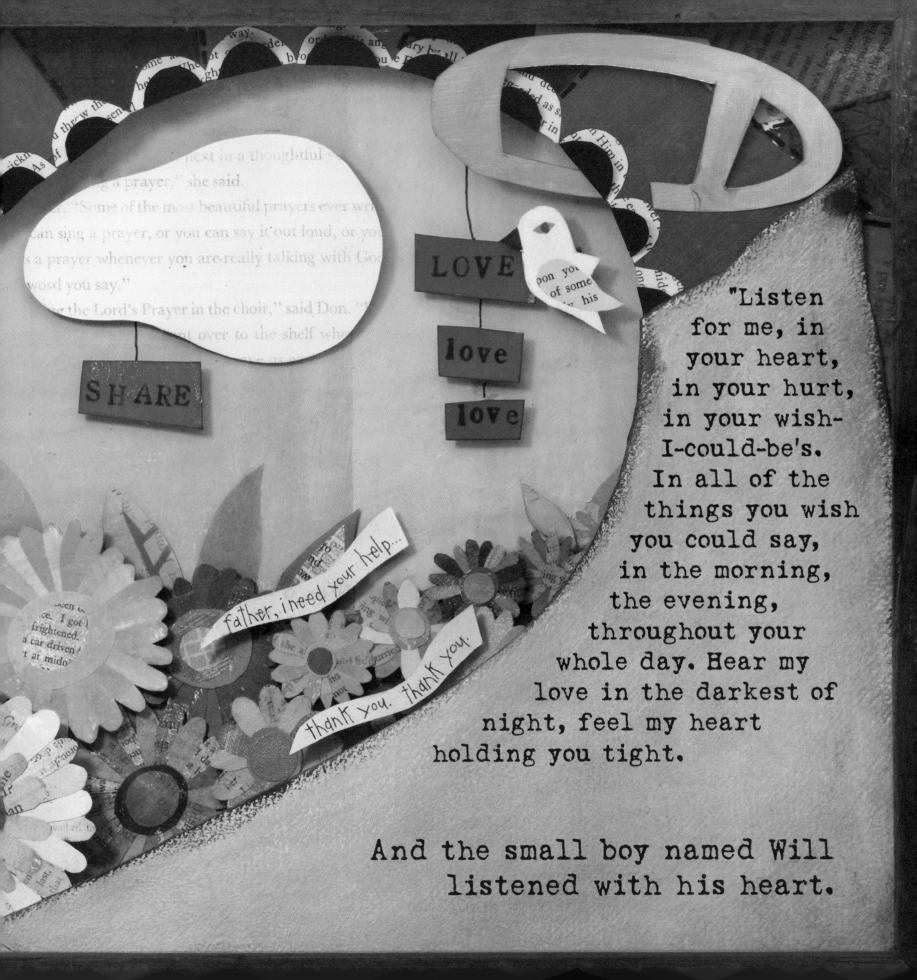

"Listen for me, in your heart, in your hurt, in your wish-I-could-be's. In all of the things you wish you could say, in the morning, the evening, throughout your whole day. Hear my love in the darkest of night, feel my heart holding you tight.

And the small boy named Will listened with his heart.

And the small boy grew. His eyes opened wide to a world that was new.

And the small voice whispered,

"Look, I am here, in an opening flower calling you near.

In the notes that you sing to make one sweet sound, in the worlds you create when there's no one around.

Give it away, the love that you hold.

"I'm here in the love you hold in your hands, in the way a snowflake falls gently to land.

Open your heart and your eyes will see, my love in the world as it's made to be."

And the small boy named Will saw with his heart.

And the small
boy grew. He trusted
in places his heart
only knew.

And the small voice
whispered,
"I'm here in your heart,
in places unseen,
your most hidden parts.
A world where love is
born and grown, where
the heart you hold is
forever known."

And the small boy named
Will believed with
his heart.

Believe

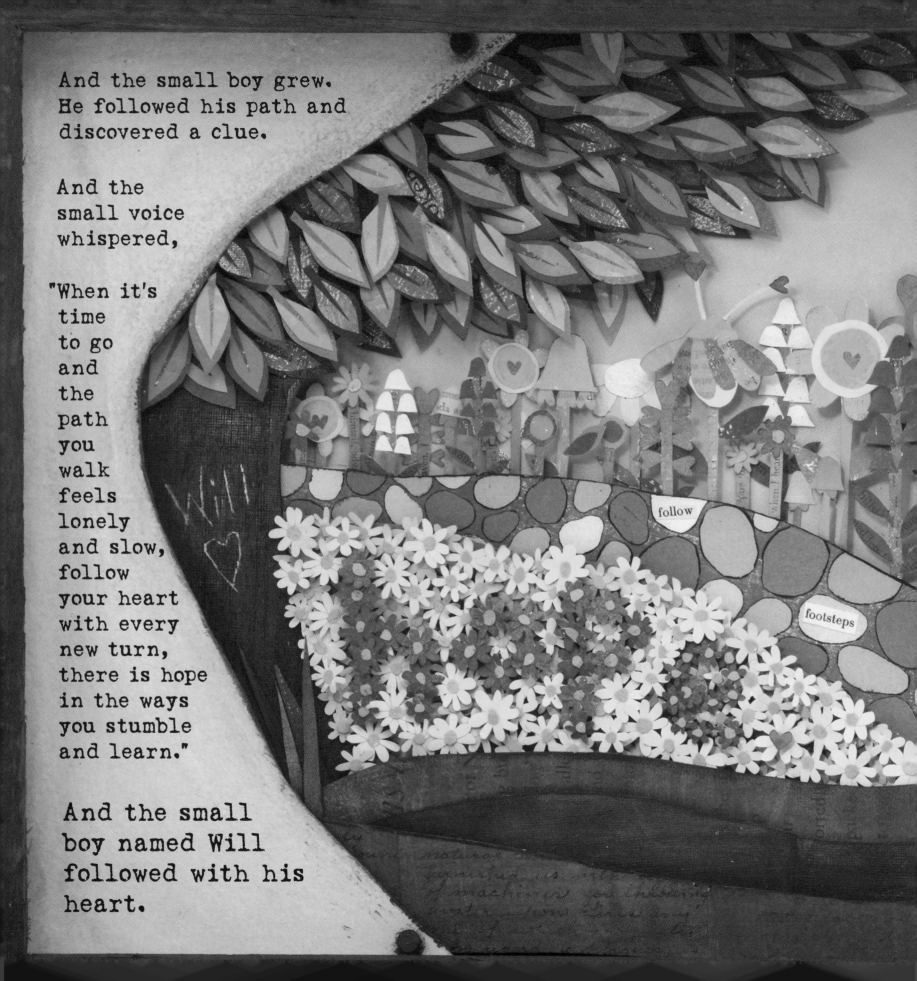

And the small boy grew.
He followed his path and
discovered a clue.

And the
small voice
whispered,

"When it's
time
to go
and
the
path
you
walk
feels
lonely
and slow,
follow
your heart
with every
new turn,
there is hope
in the ways
you stumble
and learn."

And the small
boy named Will
followed with his
heart.

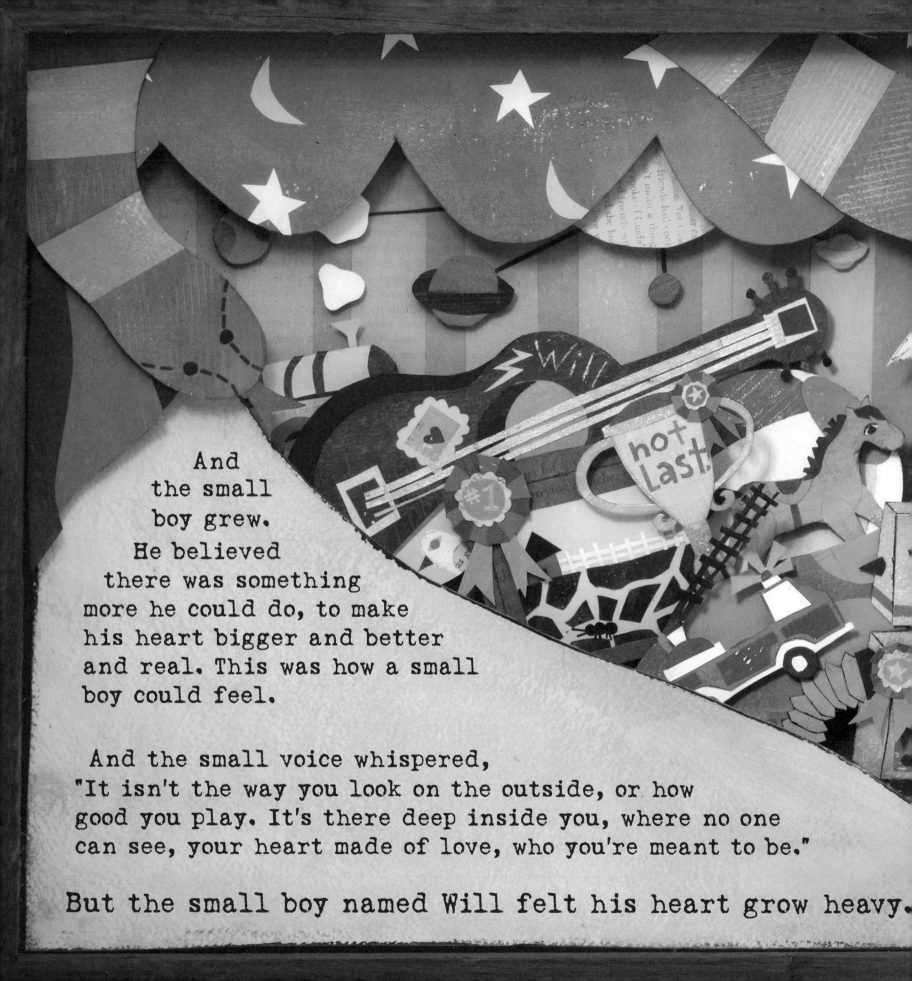

And
the small
boy grew.
He believed
there was something
more he could do, to make
his heart bigger and better
and real. This was how a small
boy could feel.

And the small voice whispered,
"It isn't the way you look on the outside, or how
good you play. It's there deep inside you, where no one
can see, your heart made of love, who you're meant to be."

But the small boy named Will felt his heart grow heavy.

And the
small boy named
Will grew lost in
his words, lost in the
things he said and he
heard. Lost in his
rights and lost in his
wrongs, lost in the
ways he wished he
belonged.

And the small voice
whispered,

"Your love grows apart
when words are
spoken without a
soft heart."

The small boy
named Will felt
his heart hurt.

LOST

boy named Will.
green pants
yellow shirt
broken heart

And the lost boy named Will hid all of his hurt. He buried his heart like a seed in the dirt.

And the small voice whispered, "Hand it to me, the hurt deep inside that no one can see. Give it away, the hurt you can't show and watch as your heart of love starts to grow."

And the small boy named Will felt his heart forgive.

The small boy grew tall as his hurt became small, for the love in his heart was there after all.

And the small voice whispered,

"You are never alone. The love in your heart will guide your heart home."

And the tall boy named Will felt his heart grow light. He stood on his path at the edge of the night.

And, so it was on this one day, a tall boy named Will found his way. Found words that wrapped around his heart, and the love he held from the very start.

And the small voice whispered, "You are loved. It's true. Always and forever. My love inside of you."

And the lost boy named Will was found.

my

love

is

your

home.

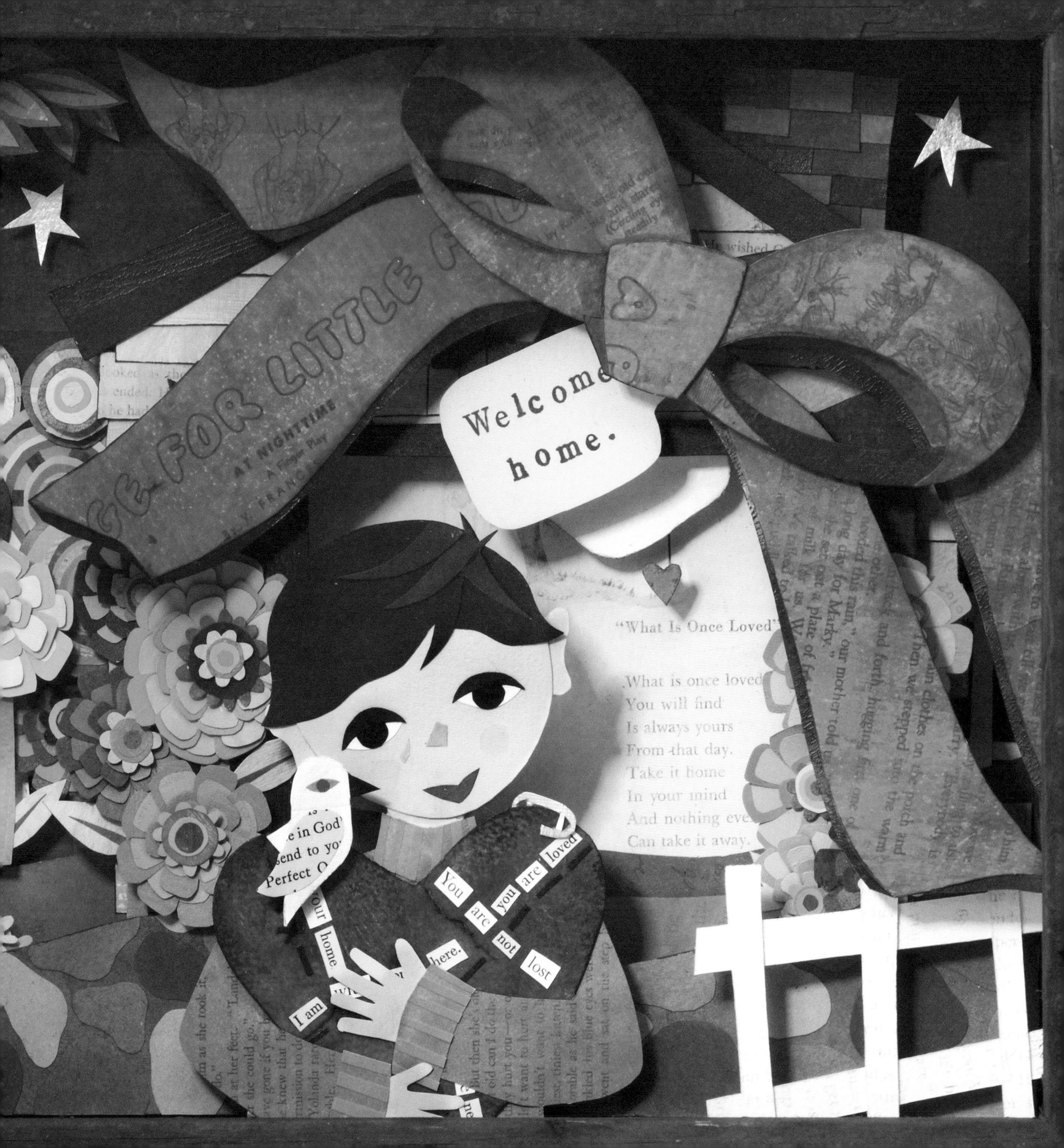

Welcome home.

"What Is Once Loved"

What is once loved
You will find
Is always yours
From that day.
Take it home
In your mind
And nothing ever
Can take it away.

You are not lost
You are loved

I am

And the found boy did love. He found in
his heart, one faithful, white dove.

And the small voice whispered,
"In your heart you're made real. Your
heart is the place where you grow and
heal. It's not when you're out or whether
you're in, it's not when you lose or just
when you win. The very thing that sets
you apart is the love made real
inside your own heart."

And the found boy
named Will felt his
heart grow
real.

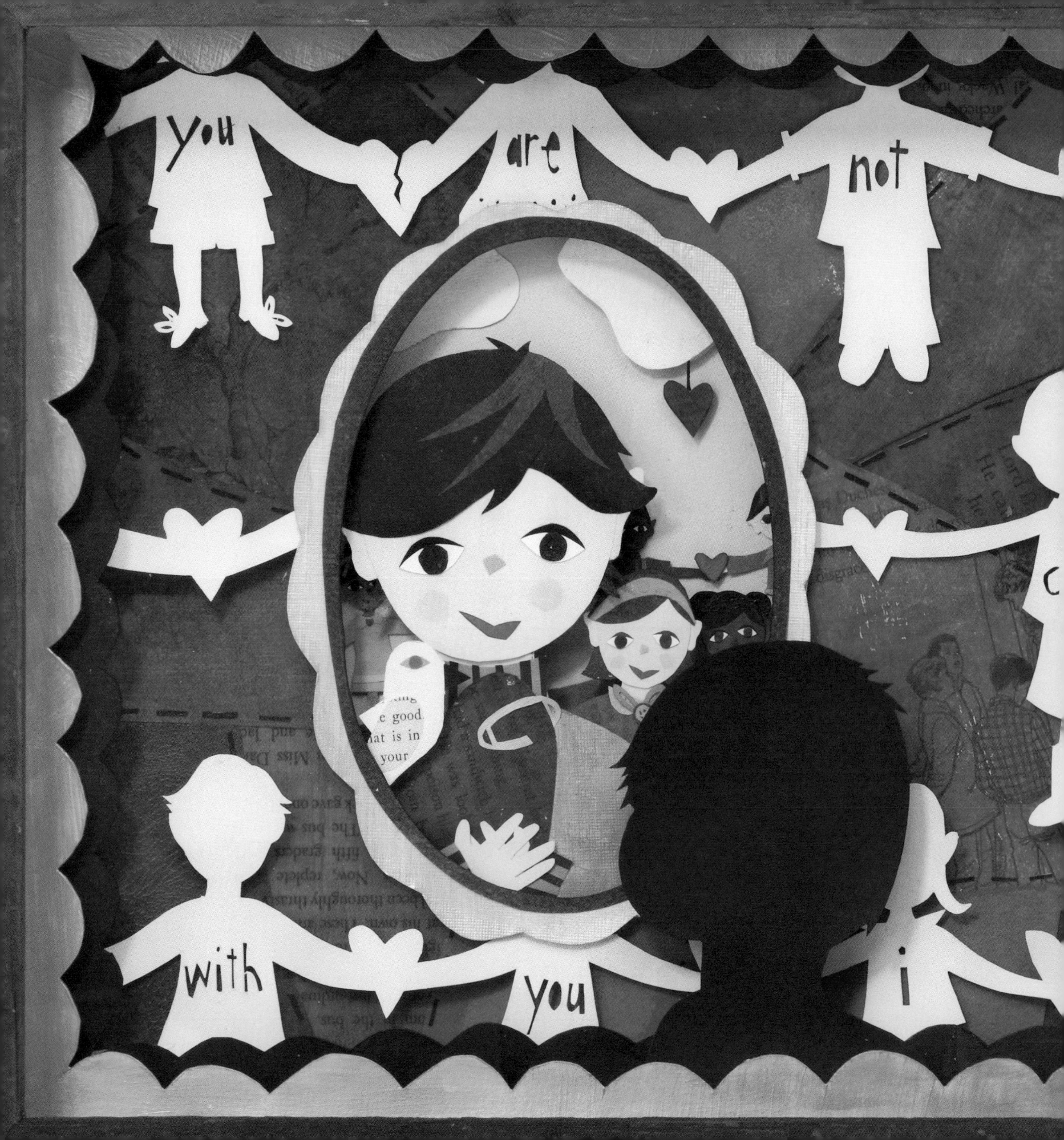
you
are
not
with
you
i

alone

i

am

And the
real boy grew
friends, hearts
that love
from beginning
to end.

And the small voice
whispered,
"Reflect what I see
in the hearts they were
given, their love
meant to be."

And the real
boy named Will
felt his heart
care.

hurt

too.

friend

And the caring boy grew bright. His heart could be seen on the darkest of nights.

And the small voice whispered,

"Your heart is a light creating a path for the lost in the night. Creating a love that longs to be seen, past the night sky, outside of a dream. And when your heart shines, when your love is aglow, a heart can see love they may not yet know."

And the caring boy named Will felt his heart shine.

hing to fear in
nothing to fear
at the silly preten
laug such
erty o want in
as we know thi
the idea of evil
King
Saviou
Christ
Yet eve
Spirit in

And the shining boy grew a gift
from his heart, a gift to share,
a gift to take part.

And the small voice whispered,

"Your heart opened wide,
reveals the gift, you hold
deep inside. A love so big,
so vast and real,
a love that
longs
to
reach
and
heal."

And
the
boy
who
shined
shared
his gift
with the
world.

I Love You

To: the
world
From:

o help
cure is
any ailme
THE BROKEN
scientist
leader
teacher
healer
artist

And the boy
who shined,
the boy
who shared,
the boy
who loved,
the boy
who cared,
The boy
who held
inside
his heart,
a gift
of love
from the
very start,
grew love
that spread
from small
to big,
found love
that comes
when we forgive.

And the small voice
whispered from deep
inside,

"Your love
is a gift
you cannot
hide.

Your heart
was made to
give and
grow, to
share and
teach so
all hearts
know...

You are loved,
You are loved,
You are
never
alone.
It is your heart
that is
your home."

And the tall
boy named Will
loved with all
of his heart.

And the boy who loved
with all of his heart
grew wings that carried
him back to the start,
grew love so big, so deep
and vast, the pin
that held it could
no longer last.

And the small voice
whispered,
"You are loved. It's true.
Always and forever.
My gift of love
is you."

And the love he gave
to the world grew.
And grew.

And
grew.

Forever
and ever.
It's true.
Always
And forever.

The love
inside of you.

The illustrations in this book were created
using vintage and discarded books on the
subjects of God and love; stories that
embodied the ideas of journey and longing,
hope and trust. The pages from these books
were then hand painted and each piece of
illustration was handcut, bringing together
the many words and voices spoken from the
pages inside these forgotten books.

It is our many stories combined that create
His one true story of Love. May we find our
hearts here.

How to share your ♥

1. pick someone to love.

2. cut out your paper ♥.

3. write words of love.

...riqn.
i wish i didn'...
use such med...
words tod...
Will you...
forg...
b...

Tiny,
am sorry you
were sad. Can
i help?

Jenny,
i was
wrong.

forgive
me.

4. decorate your ♥.
5. pin your ♥ on the person.
6. Love others as you are loved. ♥

God's c...
...ly make ...

billy,
...n we be
...nds?

sam,
i wish we were
friends
i miss ...

of King...
...nly...

There is ..son of Jona...

...an and he saw that he was

...nt only to be kind to you. I
rly. I want you to live with me

...ved with King David, and
...nathan.

A new laugh rose
nd him waddled tw
ucky. Marvelous
ed pink and wearin
other had struggle
ucky and Lucky s
s going on about t
hem into line with s
"He has been train
oster whispered to

...jose had to
quick nud

May you know that God loves you. May you know that His love lives in you. May God's love shine through you. May you know are part that you story. of His be a word, May you called a word Love. May you find your way home when you get lost. May you Know that God's love is bigger than your mistakes. May you remember home. May you remember Love. Remember. ♡

remember

you are brave.

the end

you're not alone.

Then the King said:
"A beautiful face is of littl
less there is beauty of character
we shall not decide this impo
for three days."

slipper will dance
the right one

THE GIFT